Some insects have four wings, some have two wings and some have no wings. How many wings have butterflies and moths got?

The wings are not joined together, but they move together when the butterfly flies.

Swallowtail Butterfly

The front wings do most of the work. If they are damaged, the butterfly may not be able to fly properly.

If the back wings are damaged, the butterfly can still fly.

Butterflies and moths have four wings.

Looking at wings

Red Underwing Moth

Oleander Hawk Moth

Walnut Moth

When butterflies rest, they usually close their wings above their backs.

When moths rest, they fold their wings over their backs, or spread them out flat.

Common Blue Butterfly

The wings of a butterfly or moth are often one colour on the outside and a different colour on the inside.

Privet Hawk Moth

When butterflies and moths rest, the colour of the outside of their wings makes it hard for enemies to see them.

Lappet Moth

Scallop Shell Moth

Small Skipper Butterfly

4

USBORNE FIRST NATURE
BUTTERFLIES
AND MOTHS

Games in this book

1. Hunt the little green caterpillar

Can you find 11 caterpillars like this in the book?

Make the butterfly move

Hold the book like this.

...ght hand corner ...es over fast.

watch here

Looking at butterflies and moths

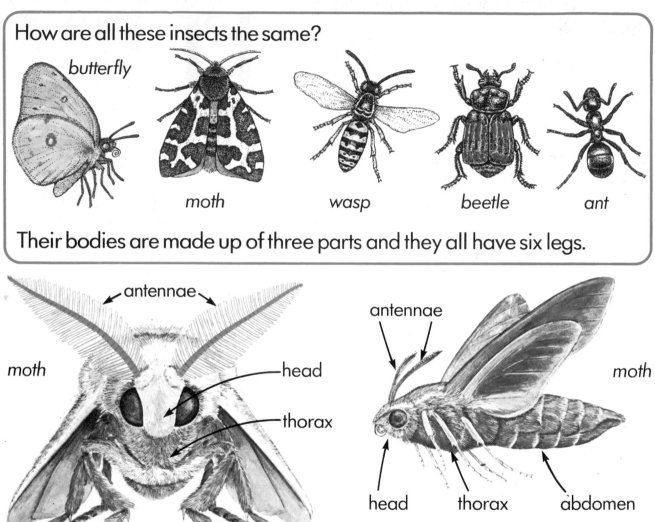

How are all these insects the same?

butterfly

moth   *wasp*   *beetle*   *ant*

Their bodies are made up of three parts and they all have six legs.

moth

antennae

head

thorax

moth

antennae

head   thorax   abdomen

Butterflies and moths have hooks on their feet for holding on tight. They feel and smell with their long antennae.

Behind the head is the thorax. The wings join on to the thorax. The long part of the body is called the abdomen.

Buff-tip Moth

Some butterflies look like dead leaves when they rest. They are hard to see.

Some moths look like twigs when they rest. It is hard for enemies to see them.

What makes the colours on their wings?

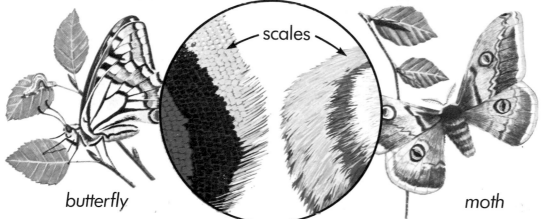

scales

butterfly

moth

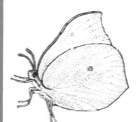

Brimstone Butterfly

Red Admiral Butterfly

The wings are covered with coloured or shiny scales. If you touch the wings the scales will rub off.

Grayling Butterfly

Green Hairstreak Butterfly

Monarch Butterfly

5

Keeping warm and feeding

Butterflies and moths need to be warm for their bodies to work properly. When the air is cold, they rest.

Butterflies warm up in the sun.

Titania's Fritillary

The dark parts of the wings warm up quickly. Butterflies from cold countries often have dark colours on their wings.

Flannel Moth

Moths are often very hairy. The hairs on their bodies help to keep them warm at night.

Elephant Hawk Moth

Moths often shiver before they fly. The shivering helps to warm up their bodies.

Butterflies and moths do not eat to grow larger.
They use food to make heat inside their bodies.
Heat makes energy. This keeps their bodies working.

*Hummingbird
Hawk Moth*

Moths and butterflies drink
a sweet liquid from flowers.
This liquid is called nectar.

They drink nectar through
a long tube called
a proboscis.

proboscis

*Union Jack
Butterfly*

Some butterflies
can taste
with their feet.

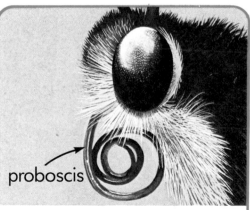

*Lime
Hawk Moth*   sap

Moths may drink sap from
trees or damaged plants.

proboscis

When butterflies and moths
are not feeding, their
proboscis is curled up.

A butterfly's day

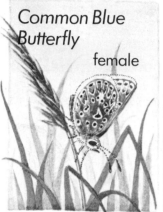

Common Blue Butterfly
female

1. The butterfly rests at night when it is cold.

2. When the sun comes out, she warms up.

3. She looks for a place to lay her eggs.

4. She lays her eggs on a special plant.

A moth's night

Privet Hawk Moth

male

1. The moth hides in the day.

2. At dusk he shivers to warm himself up.

3. He flies away to find a female.

4. He drinks some nectar from a flower.

5. She warms up again in the sun.

6. Now she is warm enough to fly away.

7. She lands on a flower to drink nectar.

8. When it gets dark and cold, she hides.

5. Now it is very cold so he rests.

6. When it gets warmer, he flies away.

7. He finds a female and mates with her.

8. When it gets light, he hides.

Finding a partner

The most important thing that a butterfly or moth has to do is to find a partner for mating. When a female has mated she will lay her eggs.

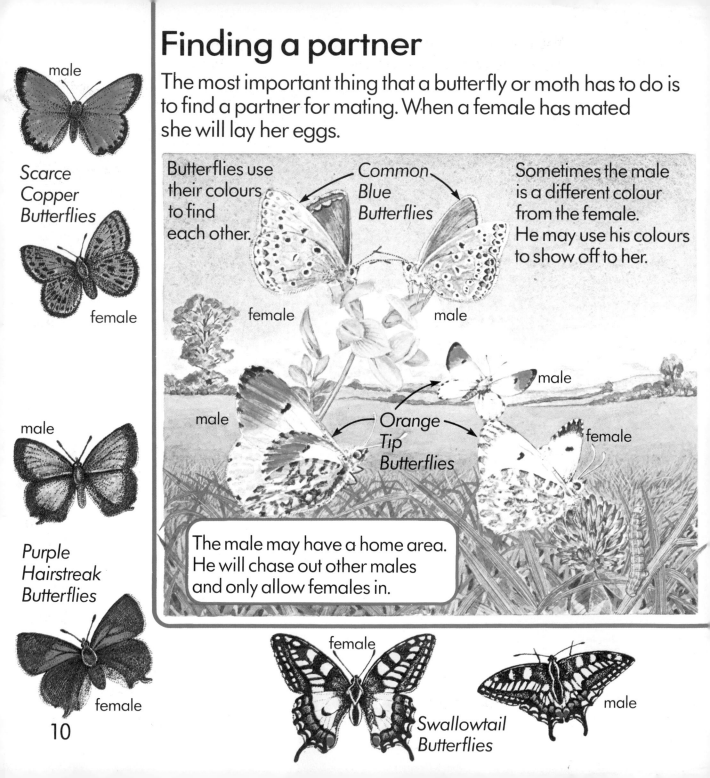

male

Scarce Copper Butterflies

female

male

Purple Hairstreak Butterflies

female

Butterflies use their colours to find each other.

Common Blue Butterflies

female

male

Sometimes the male is a different colour from the female. He may use his colours to show off to her.

male

male

Orange Tip Butterflies

female

The male may have a home area. He will chase out other males and only allow females in.

female

male

Swallowtail Butterflies

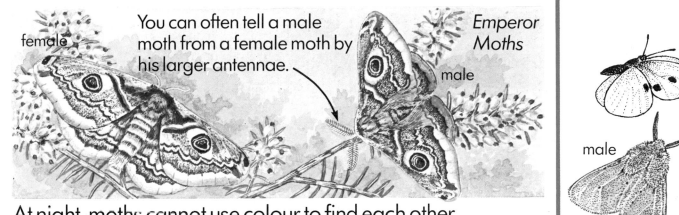

You can often tell a male moth from a female moth by his larger antennae.

female

Emperor Moths

male

At night, moths cannot use colour to find each other.
Instead the male finds the female by her scent.
Each kind of moth has a different scent.

male

Muslin Moths

female

The female gives off a special scent to attract a male.

Gypsy Moths

The male uses his feathery antennae as scent nets. He can smell a female from far away.

male

Hag Moths

female

Oak Eggar Moths

male

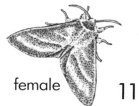

female

11

Mating and laying eggs

A pair of butterflies may play together before they mate.
This is called courtship.

The male is holding
the antennae
of the female
between
his wings.

antennae

The female uses
her antennae to
smell a scent
on the wings
of the male.

*Grayling
Butterfly*

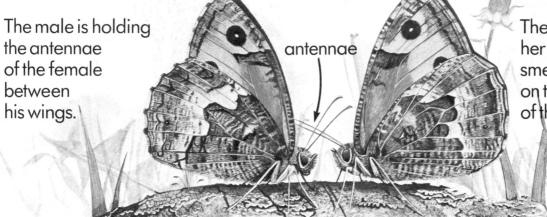

When butterflies or moths mate, they join their abdomens together.
A bag of sperm passes from the male to the female.
The sperm joins with eggs inside the female.

male

female

If they are
frightened
by an enemy,
they sometimes
fly away
joined together.

*Clouded Yellow
Butterfly*

abdomen

A female may have hundreds of eggs inside her. She will lay her eggs when she has mated.

Nettle leaf

eggs

Bulrush Wainscot Moth

abdomen

Map Butterfly

A butterfly or moth usually lays her eggs on a special plant. She can lay lots of eggs together, or one egg at a time.

This moth lays each egg inside a Bulrush. She makes holes in the stem with spines on the end of her abdomen.

Leopard Moth

Lackey Moth

egg

This Moth sticks her eggs round a twig.

This Moth sticks her eggs on to tree bark.

egg

Marbled White Butterfly

egg

This Butterfly lays her eggs as she flies.

The hungry caterpillar

Out of each egg comes a caterpillar. It eats and eats, and grows and grows. When it is big enough to start changing into an adult butterfly or moth, it stops growing.

1. A moth caterpillar is inside this egg.

2. The caterpillar eats a hole in the egg and crawls out.

3. It is very hungry, so it eats the old egg shell.

4. It eats the top of the leaf. Soon the caterpillar grows too big for its skin.

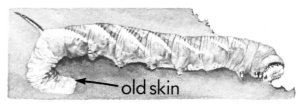

old skin

5. The skin splits and the caterpillar wriggles out. It is wearing a new skin.

Privet Hawk Moth caterpillar

6. The caterpillar eats Privet leaves. It eats and grows and eats and grows. It changes its skin three more times.

The caterpillar cannot see very well. It has twelve tiny eyes on its head. The eyes are too small for you to see.

Mouth parts for chewing.

The three pairs of front legs hold on to the food.

The five pairs of fleshy legs are called claspers. They can grip tightly to a stalk.

The caterpillar breathes through air holes in the side of its body. There is an air hole in the centre of each coloured spot.

15

Caterpillars and pupae

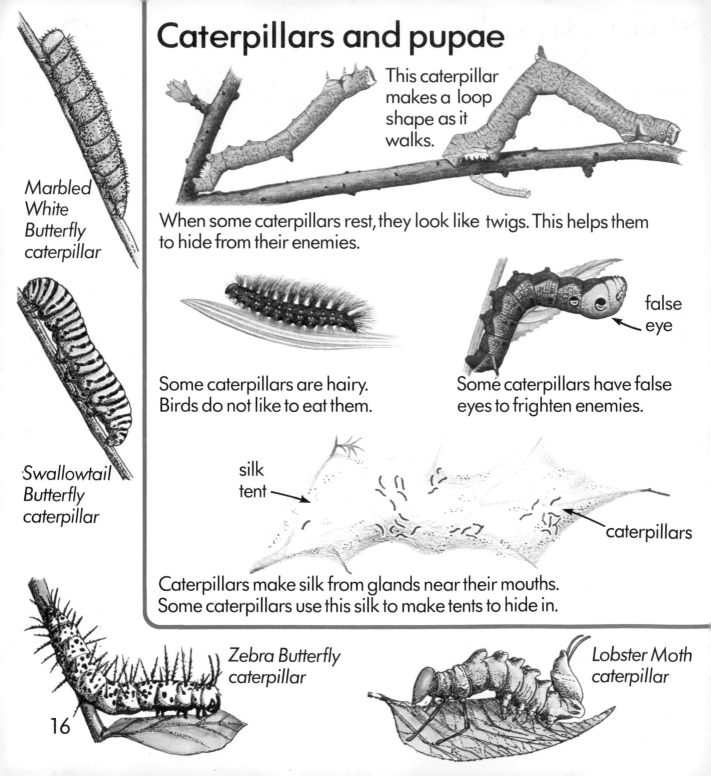

This caterpillar makes a loop shape as it walks.

When some caterpillars rest, they look like twigs. This helps them to hide from their enemies.

Marbled White Butterfly caterpillar

Swallowtail Butterfly caterpillar

Some caterpillars are hairy. Birds do not like to eat them.

false eye

Some caterpillars have false eyes to frighten enemies.

silk tent

caterpillars

Caterpillars make silk from glands near their mouths. Some caterpillars use this silk to make tents to hide in.

16

Zebra Butterfly caterpillar

Lobster Moth caterpillar

When caterpillars are fully grown, they change into pupae.

Peacock Butterfly caterpillar

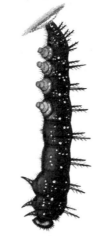

old skin

pupa

1. When this caterpillar is fully grown, it hangs upside down.

2. The caterpillar changes into a pupa inside its skin.

3. When the pupa wriggles, the skin splits. and slides up the pupa.

Cabbage White Butterfly pupa

4. The pupa skin is now hard. It has changed colour.

Some moth caterpillars bury themselves in the ground. Then they change into pupae.

silk cocoon

Some moth caterpillars spin silk cocoons around themselves. The caterpillars change into pupae inside the cocoons.

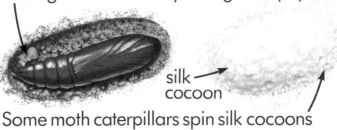

Bagworm Moth cocoon

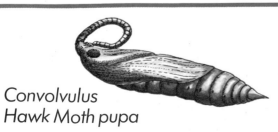

Convolvulus Hawk Moth pupa

Orange Tip Butterfly pupa

17

The magic change

Inside a pupa, a butterfly or moth is being made.

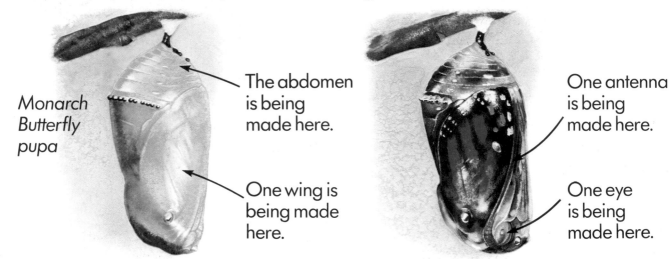

Monarch Butterfly pupa

The abdomen is being made here.

One wing is being made here.

One antenna is being made here.

One eye is being made here.

1. This pupa is two days old. A Monarch Butterfly is being made inside it.

2. The pupa is now two weeks old. The Butterfly is nearly ready to come out.

The Butterfly is pulling out its antennae, legs and proboscis.

3. The pupa skin splits. The head and legs of the Butterfly come out first.

At first,
the wings
are crumpled.

veins

The proboscis
is in
two parts.

4. The Butterfly pulls out its abdomen. It pumps blood into the veins of its wings.

5. Blood is pumping from the abdomen into the veins. This makes the wings unfold.

The two parts
of the proboscis
join together to
make a tube.

6. The Butterfly waits for its wings to dry and become stiff. Then it will be able to fly away.

How long do they live?

A butterfly or moth goes through four stages in its life. Adult butterflies and moths usually live only a few days or weeks. When they have mated and the female has laid her eggs, the adults die.

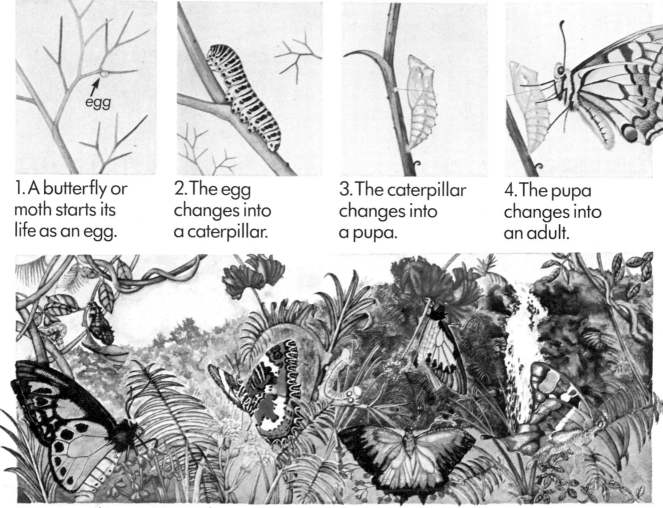

1. A butterfly or moth starts its life as an egg.

2. The egg changes into a caterpillar.

3. The caterpillar changes into a pupa.

4. The pupa changes into an adult.

In tropical countries, where the weather is always hot, a butterfly or moth often takes only a few weeks to change from an egg into an adult.

In colder countries, a butterfly or moth may take several months to change from an egg to an adult. In countries with very cold winters, they go into a deep sleep. They wake up when the weather gets warmer.

The Lackey Moth spends the winter as an egg.

The Herald Moth sleeps through the winter as an adult.

The Cabbage White Butterfly spends the winter as a pupa.

The Privet Hawk Moth spends the winter as a pupa in the soil.

The Marbled White Butterfly sleeps through the winter as a young caterpillar.

Butterflies and moths that spend part of their lives sleeping through the winter may take a year to change from an egg to an adult.

Enemies

Butterflies and moths have lots of enemies.

Birds eat them.

Spiders eat them.

Insects eat them.

At night, many moths are eaten by bats.

Some moths have ears on the sides of their bodies. They help them to hear the squeaks that bats make. If these moths hear a bat coming, they drop to the ground or try to dodge out of the way.

Blue Underwing Moth

Some butterflies and moths have special colours.
They use them to frighten away enemies.

Red Underwing Moth

If an enemy disturbs this moth, it opens
and closes its wings. The flash of red
may frighten away the enemy.

Owl Butterfly

This butterfly has false eyes on its
wings. Birds may think they are the
eyes of a dangerous animal.

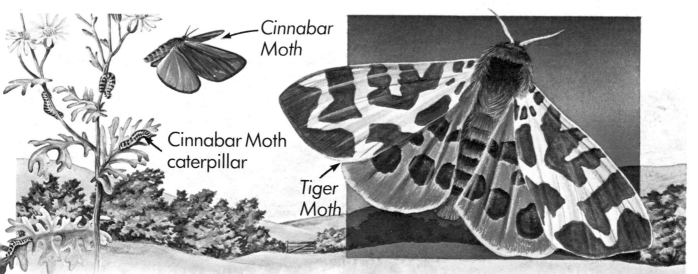

Cinnabar
Moth

Cinnabar Moth
caterpillar

Tiger
Moth

Most butterflies and moths that are red
and black, or yellow and black, taste
nasty. Birds learn to leave them alone.

At night, Tiger Moths make clicking
noises. Bats soon learn that moths
that make this noise taste bad.

Picture puzzle

There are four butterflies, three moths and four caterpillars hidden in this picture. How many can you find?

First published in 1980. Usborne Publishing Ltd, Usborne House, 83-85 Saffron Hill, London EC1N 8RT, England. © Usborne Publishing Ltd. 1990, 1980